Frank Samuel Child

Be Strong to Hope

Courage and comfort that concern the ministry of trouble

Frank Samuel Child

Be Strong to Hope
Courage and comfort that concern the ministry of trouble

ISBN/EAN: 9783337088286

Printed in Europe, USA, Canada, Australia, Japan

Cover: Foto ©Andreas Hilbeck / pixelio.de

More available books at **www.hansebooks.com**

BE STRONG TO HOPE.

COURAGE AND COMFORT

THAT CONCERN

THE MINISTRY OF TROUBLE.

BY

REV. FRANK S. CHILD.

NEW YORK:

THE BAKER & TAYLOR COMPANY, 9 BOND STREET.

MDCCCLXXXVIII.

PREFACE.

A life journey that stretches through a century, elects one to the office of precious teacher. And when one's life journey has been made in fellowship with Christ, it multiplies the worth and profit of the office. The author counts it great joy that he has been privileged to glean many helpful messages as he communed with a century old saint. The grace, the dignity, the faithfulness of this remarkable woman, have made their loyal witness through three generations. Modest, wise, generous, tireless she has lived in good obedience to her Lord. The schooling of the hundred years has been diligently mastered. And she speaks with tenderest spirit and happiest devotion concerning these same disciplines of time. It is not as text for instruction that the author inscribes this book to his aged friend. He has woven many of her interpretations of life into these pages. And the elect lady has illustrated these same messages of comfort by a character of rare beauty and merit. The author endeavors to twist these truth strands into a piece of firm, strong cordage. It is his wish and prayer that Mrs. Averill may walk a little distance with us in this the second century of her living, and that she may continue to rejoice in these familiar truths which bind her to the heart of Christ!

CONTENTS.

		PAGE.
I.	Statement,	9
II.	Pain,	19
III.	Care,	33
IV.	Worry,	47
V.	Tribulation,	61
VI.	Suffering,	73
VII.	Discipline,	87
VIII.	Adjustment,	101

STATEMENT.

STATEMENT.

"Man is born unto trouble as the sparks fly upward." That is the phraseology of Eliphaz the Temanite, and it is statement that cannot be controverted. But we want a better interpretation of it than is common to the storm-beset traveler. And it is the Bible that translates trouble into clear, vigorous, understandable terms. We turn heavenward with the psalmist and say, "Give us help from trouble, for vain is the help of man; through God we shall do valiantly." In the first place we must face the facts of the case. These facts are indicated by the statement of Eliphaz—the commonness of trouble—its variations and its continuity. It is not restricted to class or condition. "Great folks must go as well as little," said a peasant woman in Covent Garden as she learned the death of Queen Charlotte, "The Lord receive us all."

Trouble is incident to human life. There is no escape from it, and its commonness is equalled by its multiplicity. The forms of trouble are myriad. There is a kind of terror for the soul in its fitfulness and transition. "What next?" you sometimes hear the stricken, affrighted soul exclaim as one day of anguish dies and opportunity is made for the living of another. Those of us who meet disaster magnify our particular experience; and hearts that see their cherished schemes miscarry, yield them to a gloom of spirit that destroys the well-

doing of many days.   But what is harder than sickness? and with what facility disease adapts itself
to the peculiarities of diverse constitutions?   The
short sickness breaks in upon one's labor with
a carelessness that is positively hateful.   There is
no good reason why the man should be confined to
a chamber ten days while the affairs of a great estate, or the interests of a vast business centre in
him—no good reason for it as he thinks monoton-
ously, wearisomely upon the thing, and it excites
his opposition or disgust or anger.   He is apt to
complain and give way to vexation.   The sickness
may touch the mother with a persistent grip.   How
can a mother who has a large household and innumerable tasks, ever find time to be ill?   She can't
find the time.   She will fight disease, infirmity,
weariness until they three will rise in all the strength
of outrage and frenzy and maltreat her in a way
that makes the great heart of humanity cry "mercy;"
and then the household runs itself and things speedily get into confusion worse confounded, and the
worn mother submits humbly to the oblivion of fever.
The sickness may company with youth.   That
seems sadly incongruous and contrary to rightness.
Does not the Bible tell one to rejoice in his youth? and
what chance for rejoicing when youth is crippled
and unnerved and imprisoned?   The young man
has spent honest, industrious years in the work of
preparation.   Money, time, service, energy, life, have
all gone into preparation, and he has just made

happy entrance upon his promiseful field. A storm
gathers in the east. The sky is overcast. The clouds
burst and he is borne to the ground by the fury of
tempest. Tell me a more inscrutable mystery than
that which involves itself in the enforced seclusion,
the long, painful exile, the uncertain, sorrowful
awaitings that mark these years of sickness. A
sense of in describable shame seems to clothe
the youth as with a garment—that he so young,
hopeful, laborious, well-accoutred, enthusiastic,
should be sent from the field and given over to anguishful inactivity! "Know how to wait," said
Guthlac to Ethelbald of Mercia, "and the kingdom
will come to thee; not by violence or rapine, but by
the hand of God." Is that the special teaching for
the year? God knoweth. He will explain.

But trouble is featured by a tireless continuity.
It never seems to end. There are spells of inter-
mission. But they are specious so far as the most
of us are concerned, for we have a feeling that
"something is going to happen," for the very reason
that our respite makes us realize the unnaturalness
of a troubleless day. Yes, there is no end to the
strange experience. We are born to trouble as the
sparks fly upward. Memory serves us when we
have nothing else in hand. Anticipation joins with
memory, and the two keep us in a state of enliven-
ment and misery that would be well-nigh tragic
were it not so sadly grotesque. The text, "sufficient
unto the day is the evil thereof," is one that few

people master ; "and to those who lie out of the road
of great afflictions," says Walter Scott in Guy Man-
nering, "are assigned petty vexations which answer
all the purpose of disturbing their serenity."

But we have dwelt upon these obvious facts with
all needful insistence. What shall we say as to the
significance of trouble. Is there hate, annoyance,
revenge, chance, fate in the thing, or shall we con-
strue it into wise teaching, solicitous guidance, loyal
interference, helpful stimulation? An interpretation of trouble that reflects the thought of God, has
supreme importance when you come down to practical matters. Putting God away from the spirit
or putting one's self away from God is courting darkness, failure, despair, when we face the problem of
trouble. There are men whose souls are brave—
whose hearts are purposeful. But the long-sought
opportunity evades them. They turn toward life
with mighty zeal of achievement, but sickness, circumstance, condition, negative their purpose. Life
is reduced to an experience of waiting. That is
trouble that has the somberest aspect. The man
consumes his precious vitality in feeding disease
or truckling to limitations. "Give me my task, O
God," is the prayer that daily rises in accents of
pitiful entreaty, but the even tenor of the petty,
hampered way changes not, and the man abides in
the deep shadows. Gyves are upon his wrists and
ankles. He is helpless, and yet there lives in his soul
the conviction that God has work for him to do. It is

no small matter to say hopefully to such a man, "know how to wait." Why must he tarry in the solitary chamber? He is well equipped for royal service—nevertheless it *is* his singular experience that he so strong, alert, wise, devout, must be taught through affliction. The kingdom will come to him by the hands of God when full days of preparation are recorded. Who can interpret the necessities of the spirit as the wise and loving Father?

Now we can steel ourselves against troubles and show a bold front as they assail us; but that does not rhyme with the spirit of the gospel. Stoicism is not Christianity. Stern endurance makes discord when you parallel it with glad submission. Then we can yield us to trouble with a kind of hardened passiveness that has no faith or courage or vitality in it. There is possibility that a soul may breathe the anæsthetics of despair, so that troubles produce the slightest and transientest sensations. But these methods do not commend themselves. The truth of it is that trouble cannot be evaded or intimidated or scourged. It has a ministry. How deep the impression of its service when it enters the home as the messenger of death? The child that you love laughs her love into your heart. The eyes image love—the dimpled cheek presses love as it nestles against your breast—the very lips kiss love into your life, and this beautiful, priceless child-flower withers when some disease frost hovers close to it with its deathful breath. You put the little form to rest.

"Oh God, that I were sleeping by her side!" that is your piteous outcry. But your thought gets turned heavenward. The love cords that fastened you to earth are made to relax—a realness that concerns the blessed immortality of the dead who die in the Lord takes substantial form in your life—affections are curiously and assuredly transported into the realm of the everlasting and all glorious. Your very nature is mellowed, ripened, sanctified by the subtle, precious influences of your sorrow. Behold, you are made perfect through suffering. Strange law, inscrutable fact, inevitable experience! What is this Ministry of Trouble that we may get its comfort, its inspiritment, its healthfulness and its benediction!

We have made swift statement. "We are born to trouble as the sparks fly upward." There is a certain mystification and incomprehensibleness about the matter as we give it swift and unsympathetic gaze. The score of a symphony is a complex and suggestive thing. Uneducated eyes do not read the method, motive, movement that are told by the written language of music. Solo, chorus, voice, transition, acclamation, woof of melody with warp of accompaniment; startling variations, delicate shadings, and all confused, exalted by little sharps and flats that contain infinite possibilities of discord or harmony! That same score, when perfectly interpreted, bears one throneward and prostrates the spirit before God. The score of this world-life symphony is infinitely complex and variegated. It is a study of sharps and flats with us—this inquiry concerning the Ministry of Trouble. But we are sure that the sharps and flats named troubles will all be finally adjusted to the rich and masterful melody that phrases God's glory.

PAIN.

PAIN.

"Why is my pain perpetual?" * * Jer. xv : 15.

The prophet asks a pertinent question. Pain is certainly a common thing. It comes into every life with a force and a persistency that appall us. And the words of Christ touch common life so wisely and so helpfully, that we are sure they will instruct us in this matter of pain. "We know that the whole creation groaneth and travaileth in pain together until now." There is a mystery about it that we do not attempt to solve. We simply confess its presence and operation ; then we set ourselves to the task of learning its serviceableness and applying to ourselves its unforgetable instructions. Pain, we readily see, is a sort of sentinel, warning us that the enemy approaches. The twinge in the foot or the eye means that disease or abuse is making its record. The parched lips, the inflamed stomach, the unsteady gait, the aching head, the dazed brain, the sense of shame, the feeling of desperation, the stings of conscience, these pains mean that the man has wronged himself and wronged his Creator; these pains mean that penalty has its onerous, misery-making offices. For pain is punishment; that is the derivation of the word—the Latin *pœna*— punishment. Pain, as Trench tells us, is the cor-relative of sin. The word "itself no less than the conscience of every one that is suffering it de-

clares it." Pain warns us with stern tone and firm
bearing. There is nothing timid or bashful about
it. It is never hindered by reticence or modesty.
But this is one of the minor offices of pain. It warns,
restrains, corrects, plagues. But it is pain in its
higher office that we propose to study. It has a
moral significance. Christ instructs us with marked
earnestness concerning the moral bearing of pain.

Pain of body and pain of mind—they are inti-
mately related. We do not tarry to discriminate
them; taking the economy of nature as it is pre-
sented to us, we observe that sin being a factor, pain
enters as a thing of necessity. Sunshine means
heat; storm clouds mean moisture; sin means suffering. "There is none righteous, no not one."
That helps to answer Jeremiah's inquiry, "why is
my pain perpetual?"

There is pain for self's sake. The law says that
we are to let our moderation be known unto all men.
The body is to be fostered with a wise solicitude
and consistent treatment. It is a servant. The
soul is master. The servant should never be per-
mitted to reverse this relation and gain the mastership. But that is the history when appetites and
passions control the man. The man sinks into serf-
dom. The pampered body tramples upon the rights,
privileges, powers of the soul and such disorder
brings pain into the life. Body pains and mind
pains go hand in hand. Gluttony, sensuality, they
defile the body, lead to diseases that riot with

excruciating pains and at the same time induce an irritability and a repulsion and a wretchedness of mind that make life a loathsome experience for one's self, and a hateful, weary martyrdom for one's friends. There is no respite nor relief so long as one remains in such condition of defiance. "Whatsoever a man soweth, that shall ·he also reap." When men sow to the flesh they get their woful harvest of flesh disease and physical suffering. Pain for such men is thoroughly punishment. A recent cable dispatch tells of a woman who haunted the gaming tables of Monte Carlo during the summer. She carried with her a fortune of $60,000. She was inflamed by the wickedness of this gaming hell. All sense of womanhood and decency were forfeited in her infatuation. She played with reckless hand. She tried to drown her wretchedness in wild gains ; and when her fortune was gone the degraded, frenzied creature hastened to a village near Grenoble and there became her own murderer. And this, says the record, is the seventy-sixth suicide of one Monte Carlo season. "No man can serve two masters, for either he will hate the one and love the other, or else hold to the one and despise the other." "Every tree that bringeth not forth good fruit is hewn down and cast into the fire." Just what these two sayings mean when translated into terms of pain I leave you to judge. Illustrations are too common and too tragic to require explanation. This is pain in one sense for the

self's sake. It is pain that comes as unavoidable,
righteous punishment. It is deserved, courted, made
certain. But there is pain for self's sake which is
disciplinary and educative. Choice flowers require
rank soil. It is one of the marvellous things of
plant life that rare strength, beauty, fragrance,
thrive upon the fetted rotten soil. Pain is the kind
of soil in which some of the rarest flowers of character grow. Patience, compassion, graciousness,
charity, they demand large fertilization of the pain
kind. The thirteenth chapter of I. Corinthians
makes elaborate statement of the matter. One
must live many rough experiences and weather
many hard trials before the soul manifests a dis-
position which suffereth long and is kind. It is
grand achievement when the soul has attained that
condition of life where she " doth not behave herself
unseemly ; seeketh not her own ; is not easily pro-
voked ; thinketh no evil ; rejoiceth not in iniquity ;
but rejoiceth in the truth ; beareth all things ; be-
lieveth all things ; hopeth all things ; endureth all
things." But this description signifies great measures of pain. It doesn't seem such a great task
when we first read of it, that Grace Darling, living
by the Northumberland reefs, should save life after
life through her singular ministry to distress. Why!
she could swim and her gentle heart was moved with
pity in this service for men. But that is a small and
niggard way in which to interpret it. There was
unreckonable pain in this ministry. Pains of body—

the buffeting of winds and waves, fatigue, rough usage, wounds, weakness, the strain of nerves, the shattering of muscles, the forfeiture of vital power, tremendous risks to physical life—pains of mind— eagerness, uncertainty, tension, anguish, a sympathy that was full of suffering, a determination that was toned by the largest self-abnegation, a hope that was cheered by the noblest emotion. Think of the pain which was compressed into the structure of this womanhood. Grace Darling's sister recently died. She was a plain, modest, pious woman. "Oh," said she, when people spake with her concerning the precious labor of Grace Darling, "it was just plain matter of duty, nothing for the world to talk so much about." True. But I want you to notice what it cost this brave, great woman. I want you to reckon, so far as they are reckonable, the pains endured; and then observe that this is illustrative of Christ's great law concerning pain. "Whosoever will be great among you, let him be your minister, and whosoever will be chief among you, let him be your servant. Even the son of man came not to be ministered unto, but to minister, and to *give his life* a ransom for many." This marks out the line of sufferingness. It is this pain which emphasizes its instruction day by day, that is drilling and shaping the man, the woman into fortitude, endurance, mastery. This is the kind of soil that cherishes the rarest flowers. Pain supplies the needful sustenance. Without it these rare flowers never unfold themselves and disclose their beauteousness.

B

But there is pain that must be borne for men's sake. We are part of a great scheme. The selfishness of a man antagonizes the entire body of humanity. We cannot destroy the fact that all men share our common life and destiny. We may try to ignore it, we may put ourselves into an attitude of denial, but our course makes its impression; our individuality goes for its full weight. The wires that are twisted into the massive cables of the Brooklyn bridge have as large opportunity and as good reason for denying their relation to each other and their relations to the structure, as have men the opportunity and the reason to deny their human relationships and obligations. So Christ says that we must learn the ministry of pain in our person as it bears upon the life and character of our fellows. Then said Christ unto his disciples, "It is impossible but that offences will come, but woe unto him through whom they come," Luke xvii : 1. There is a great burden of pain for us to bear. That pain holds definite relation to the work of the world. We read the brief notes which Bishop Hannington made in his journal as he crossed Africa in his last tragic missionary journey. The journal tells how he was attacked by twenty natives, overpowered and dragged a long distance. It tells how he was stripped and nobbed; how he was thrown into a hut thas was loathsome with vermin and decayed matter. It tells how he lay there ill and helpless, while drunken natives and derisive guards peered into his confinement. On the eighth day he makes this brief last pathetic note : " No news ; a hyena howled all night, smelling a sick man ; hope he will not have me yet." And shortly afterward the brave, faithful bishop was slaughtered. Here is a narrative of pain that moves the soul with mighty impulse. The moral impression of such teaching is incalculable. We cannot tell what work of truth teaching it did for these poor deluded savages. We are fain to believe that such char- acter must have rayed its brightness into the ob- scurity of some curious, observant hearts. But we can pronounce with considerable definiteness con- cerning the moral impression of this suffering as it bears upon Christendom. A throb of sympathy surges through the world. Men are strangely taught the power of Christian purpose. Instead of reproach and vindictiveness on the part of the Church, the call sounds for recruits to martyrdom. The heathen must be taught the way of life, and so it results that a company of men, fired with loyalty to Christ, make offering of themselves and prepare to pene- trate into these dark places of the world and suffer for the sake of ignorant and godless nations.

And there is pain that must be borne for God's sake. There is such a thing as witness to the truth. Conflict assumes a sort of impersonal character. We stand for right. The personal element is small and obscure. A certain course, a specified attitude, are synonymous with right. That induces perse-

cution. Pain, as Bushnell says, "becomes the in-
terpreter of wrong." "Remember the word that I
said unto you. The servant is not greater than
his Lord. If they have persecuted me, they will
also persecute you."—John xv : 20. This is pain that
is avoidable. We can shirk the work. We can refuse the duty. Even Christ insists upon the free-
ness with which the soul elects itself to such suffering. When the angry crowd, led by Judas, came
to seize our Saviour, one of his companions drew
his sword and smote off the ear of the high priest's
servant. "Then said Jesus unto him, put up again
thy sword into his place." * * * "Thinkest thou
that I cannot now pray to my father and he shall
presently give me more than twelve legions of
angels."—Matt. xxvi : 32 and 33. But he did not wish
to avoid the suffering. He stood for truth. Pain
was a large, mysterious factor in his mission. He
must suffer. As we are his disciples the same course
opens to us. "Inquisitor Titelmann heard that
a certain schoolmaster was addicted to reading
the Bible. (This was in Holland, 1561, when Philip
II. was king.) Titelmann examined the schoolmaster and discovered that he was a heretic. He
commanded him to recant. Schoolmaster refused.
"Do you not love your wife and children?" asked
the inquisitor. "God knows that if the whole world
were of gold and my own, I would give it all only
to have them with me." "You have then only to
renounce the error of your opinions," said Titel-

mann. "Neither for wife, children, nor all the world can I renounce my God and religious truth," answered the prisoner. So the schoolmaster was strangled and then burned at the stake. This is pain for God's sake. It is unswerving attestation to the divineness of the gospel. Here is instance where we join with Christ in paying the cost of a regenerated world. "Are ye able to drink of the cup that I shall drink of, and to be baptized with the baptism that I shall be baptized with?" Jesus put this question to the two men that sought preëminence in his kingdom. They say unto him, "we are able." And he saith unto them, "Ye shall drink indeed of my cup, and be baptized with the baptism that I am baptized with."—Matt. xx : 22 and 23. The pain comes—not as righteous visitation upon us for *our* sin, not as penal experience for the iniquities of ancestors. The pain scourges us as witness. In our small way we stand for right. Opposition and antagonism aim at this or that man as he embodies truth. The hero may abdicate his position. He may renounce the principle that phrases itself in his person. But so long as he lives the truth, and holds forth the word of life, so long must he share the pain that makes him a target. Insult and innuendo, rough assault and malicious contrivance, scorn, abuse, cruelty, harassment, fraud, deceit, injury, wounding, these are modes and instruments which do the wicked work of persecution.

It is put with thorough distinctness. We must
suffer for self's sake. God will bring every man into
judgment for the deeds done in the body, whether
they be good or whether they be evil. We must
suffer for men's sake. As vicar we must bear the
pains that threaten their dire consequences upon
our loved ones, and upon the great social order of
which we are part. "Whosoever shall not take up
his cross and follow me, cannot be my disciple."
We must suffer for God's sake. "Ye have heard
that it has been said 'an eye for an eye, and a tooth
for a tooth;' but I say unto you, resist not evil, but
whosoever shall smite thee on thy right cheek,
turn to him the other also."—Matt. v : 38 and 39.
"Blessed are ye when men shall revile you and persecute you, and shall say all manner of evil against
you falsely for *my* sake. Rejoice and be exceeding
glad for great is your reward in heaven." The
pain must come. It takes infinite forms. Disease,
sorrow, error, work, assault, death, hatred, poverty,
crime, persecution, defeat. Pain comes through a
myriad of channels. But it is always pain, and it
is nothing but pain. It belongs to this world estate.
We read a part of its significance as it does its task
of purification and stimulation. And we learn the
noble attitude of soul concerning pain as we follow
the Saviour through his toilsome, painful journey
from the manger to the cross. "Father, forgive
them, for they know not what they do." Brave,
invincible pain-bearing; unselfish, compassionate

pain-bearing; Christ frames the full law through the unutterable work on Calvary.

Friends, let us find the help and impulse that lie hidden in life's pain. Let us affirm with Conrad, king of Germany, "I know what I owe to Jesus; I will go wheresover he shall call me." Then shall we seasonably enter that home land in which, says the author of Revelation, "there shall be no more pain."

CARE.

CARE.

" Be not anxious."—Matt. vi : 34.

There are certain limited regions of the tropics in which the necessities of life are reduced to the minimum. The climate is torrid, so that the natives do not need any wardrobe. The soil is prodigal— the bread-fruit, the banana, the cocoanut, supplying all essential nourishment. The habits of the inhabitants are simple and primitive, so that life does not demand any show, pomp, extravagance. And the people exist without cares. When we fret under the friction of our complicated, burdensome life, we look with some envy and longing to this state of nature. And occasionally we find men who resist the pressure of our vast artificial system and flee them to the desert or the wilderness. They purpose to avoid the wear and work of the great world and give themselves to ease or study, or meditation, or rebellion.

We have all felt the strength of such desire and purpose. As we have multiplied cares and activities, we have all longed to go into retreat for a season and comfort ourselves with quiet and release us from the restless, dominant spirit of this present world life. The man whose interests and relations are vast and intricate, has at times a terrible sense of

such necessity. His farms, and stocks, and merchan-
dise, and ships, and buildings, they mean so much
care to him that they put other and better things out
of sight and out of mind. He may say, as did A. T.
Stewart concerning his enormous business, " Positively everything to be done has somebody else to do
it besides myself." But the fact remains that one man
stands at the helm. His hand has supreme control.
The care of the thing reverts to him. The woman
whose household tasks seem to multiply with each
day's coming, whose sympathies, and corrections,
and counsels, and arbitrations, and ingenuities, and
affections are all the time demanded by her little
complex, energetic, busy, company of children and
relations—how does she fling herself down to rest
with unutterable sense of burdens, responsibilities,
tasks? If she could only go into retirement for some
still, calm hours, how she would gather herself anew
for the work and go to meet her cares with a force
of mastership that seems unconquerable. And the
same deep desire quickens in the heart of all men who
enter with serious, earnest, noble purpose into the
vast work of the world. Our cares take such shape
and increase their number with such unreckonable
rapidity that we are often staggered by them ; and
on occasion we yield to their force with a sense of
defeat that is sadly humiliating. Cares make up a
large part of life. Cares share in the moulding of
character. Cares have such close relation to the
daily narrative of our living that we are sure to

find how Christ pronounced upon the subject with particularity and wisdom.

It isn't avoidance of care that the Master recommends. It isn't "take no thought for your life." That is a mis-translation. "Be not anxiously careful for your life;" or "Be not anxious for your life." It is an excess of thoughtfulness—it is an extravagance of carefulness that is reprobated and condemned. The Master doesn't expect that we shall shirk the cares of this world. Men must eat, drink, clothe themselves, engage in business, honor domestic relations, share in the ministry to sickness, poverty, distress,—and these things signify a certain burden of responsibility. "Am I my brother's keeper?" The affirmative reply to this query put by Cain involves a series of cares that touch the living of every day. We don't like it, that our companions, acquaintances, fellow creatures, are put into our keeping. It isn't comfortable to be told that our word, our act, our life, has much to do with the goodness or the badness of neighbors and society ; but such is the fact and it brings cares into our personal experience. We sometimes try to wash our hands of the evil courses and consequences which imperil people. We imitate Pilot. We refuse to countenance the wickedness, but we do not refuse our tacit consent to the proceedings. "When Pilot saw that he could prevail nothing * * he took water and washed his hands before the multitude, saying, "I am innocent of the blood of this just person; see ye to it."—Matt. xxvii. But Pilot consented to this crime against high heaven. He could not wash his hands of it. Christ was Pilot's prisoner. He was committed to Pilot's care. And tradition follows Pilot in his anguishful remorse to the distant lake Pilatus, where he is said to have smothered his agony in tempestuous waters.

The cares come. They belong to life. They have their part in the structure of manhood. But we pervert them or misinterpret them, so that they work us injury and ruin.

First we mark the warning in respect to cares; "Take heed to yourselves, lest at any time your heart be overcharged with surfeiting and drunkenness, and *cares* of this life."—Luke xxi: 34. When cares multiply to such an extent, when they assume such importance that we cannot give first thought and first love to God, and right then we are guilty of this law of Christ. That explains the defalcation of such a man as Gray. He was reputed honest. He was counted religious. But he was ambitious in respect to a prodigal style of living. The home establishment and the yacht establishment, personal expenditures, family expenditures, charitable expenditures, they made enormous drain upon his salary, income, capital. He was careful about many things, but it was carefulness that had little virtue about it. It was a carefulness that centered in show, dress, pleasure, indulgence. It was a carefulness that pushed *right* out of the plan and drove Christ out of the soul. "Take heed to yourselves lest at any time your heart be overcharged with the cares of this life."

We also mark the uselessness of anxiety : "Which of you by taking thought can add one cubit to his stature?" observed the Master. He was speaking to the end that we should feel our God dependence. God created us. He set us in this system of natural and spiritual laws which holds us with its vice-like grip. It is only through an appropriation of the gifts of God that we attain any strength and mastery. We are under complete subjection to the laws of life. " If," continues Christ, "ye then be not able to do that which is least, why take ye thought for the rest?" If we cannot say "grow" and then grow in response to the command, but find ourselves obliged to submit to God's laws, which laws shape things into wise form for us,— why should we worry about the innumerable details of personal life and world life? We have simply to walk in appointed ways, do the appropriate work, use the ordained means, and we are sure of the result. A profound and thorough trust in the truth of God gives no opportunity for the play of anxiety. Care, a wise, tender, affectionate concern for the things of life, is legitimate because such care is essential to the best living and the noblest achievement ; but thought that is toned with fear and fever, thought that is unnerved by fret and ferment, thought that is moved by terror and despair,

that serves no good purpose in the life.   It hampers
the man, it curses the man, it destroys the man.

We also mark the statement that cares are
apt to obstruct the flow of right life.   This is put
into form by the parable of the sower.   Some of the
seed sowed by the sower "fell among thorns ; and
the thorns sprang up with it and choked it."   The
seed which fell among thorns, says Christ, "are they
which, when they have heard, go forth and are
choked with cares,   *   *   and bring no fruit to
perfection."—Luke viii : 7–14.   There must be a
reasonable limit to the cares which we assume.
The chief end of man is to glorify God. We glorify
God by carving our human nature into the likeness
of Christ.   When we have so much to do in the
way of making money, attending to business, in-
dulging pleasures, gratifying tastes, that we leave
little time or no time for the concerns of the soul,
we are breaking Christ's law and obstructing the
flow of right life.   It is called hard for rich men,
prominent men, busy men, to become good men.
There are apologies which explain the saying, for
men of large affairs seem to require more than the
twenty-fonr hours a day.   But it is against this very
devotedness and concentration that the words of
Christ are aimed.   Business and pleasure that inter-
fere with good character and good growth are oppos-
ed to the gospel and faith of Jesus.   If cares are so
numerous and burdensome that they distract the man
and wean him from God, they should be lessened or

rejected. We are to bring forth fruit to perfection. Anything that contradicts such result must receive the stamp of disapproval. With what force of incident does the Master emphasize this teaching? Here is the simple narrative as told by Luke (x : 38–41 :) " Now it came to pass, as they went, that he (Christ) entered into a certain village ; and a certain woman named Martha received him into her house. And she had a sister called Mary, which also sat at Jesus' feet, and heard his word. But Martha was cumbered about much serving, and came to him, and said, Lord, dost thou not care that my sister hath left me to serve alone? bid her therefore that she help me. And Jesus answered and said unto her, Martha, Martha, thou art careful and troubled about many things ; but one thing is needful ; and Mary hath chosen that good part, which shall not be taken away from her." Martha was thinking too much about entertainment that appealed to the lower nature. She was anxious concerning the common things of the home life. And her anxiety destroyed her spiritual balance. She didn't pay good attention to the precious truths that Christ spread before them. She failed to profit by the gracious presence that was rich in all helpfulness. And our Lord rebuked her for such mistake and negligence. But the tragic aspect of this thing is framed by one of our Lord's parables. "A certain man made a great supper and bade many "—(Luke xiv : 16–20. ;) " and sent his servant at supper time to say to them

c

that were bidden, come, for all things are now
ready. And they all with one consent began to
make excuse. The first said unto him, I have
bought a piece of ground, and I must needs go and
see it; I pray thee have me excused. And another
said, I have bought five yoke of oxen, and I go to
prove them; I pray thee have me excused. And
another said, I have married a wife, and therefore
I cannot come. * * Then this master of the
house was wroth." "I say unto you that none of
those men which were bidden shall take of my supper." It was care that these men used as excuse
for absence. "I have too much money to join the
Master and be a Christian." "I am too busy with
common affairs to sit at the Lord's table and company with His people." That was the meaning of
the excuse. And it is the excuse that some of us
make to-day. And it is an excuse whose tragic
issue is marked with woeful certainty. "None of
those men who were bidden shall take of my supper." The kingdom of heaven is closed forever to
those foolish, defiant men who give themselves to
care and refuse the invitation of God.

We observe then as the result of this care
study, that Christ forbids all care that has any
element of fret, worry, fear, and distrust about it.
This doesn't mean that we are to idle away the
day, that we are not to plan for the future, that
we are excused from doing our very best. This
doesn't mean that we are to take our chances with

life and make no effort toward competency and comfort. It doesn't mean that we are not to face toil, pain,
trial, sorrow, loss, calamity, death. But it does
mean that we are to repose upon the Fatherhood of
God ; that the Father's knowledge of our needs is
perfect ; that His great world scheme and His special
dealing of providence will meet the necessities of
every case with fitness, precision, vigor, efficiency.
It is a rich and sublime trust that is taught by
Christ concerning care. The care we cannot evade
or dismiss. But the anxiety of care, the tremendous factor of mental wear and anguish—*that* we
must press from this life or we are disobedient to
the Word of God and bereft of the precious ministry
of the Spirit.

Now note the bearing of such instruction upon
the experience of the day. What is it that pencils
the lines upon our faces and chisels the furrows
upon our brows ? It isn't work, it isn't age. It is
the endless fret of care. The farmer fears that his
seeds will rot in the ground, or his grains will die
of thirst, or the winds will blight his fruits, or disease destroy his cattle. And the manufacturer
fears that the price of labor will rise and the profit
of trade lessen. He thinks that the strength of
competition will increase, while the demands of the
people will grow small. And the merchant, he has
large stock and the markets vary. A change in one
way brings him fortune ; a change in the other way
brings him bankruptcy. Then there are storms,

illnesses, fires, treacheries, miscalculations, floods, wars, monopolies, legislations,—a thousand things to complicate business. And business agents are all human ; they are subject to indescribable and unreckonable variations and influences.

Well, there is a great deal in life to make us feel the dubiousness and the contradictoriness of the future. And Christ teaches a man *how* to meet these things with brave spirit, right spirit, invincible spirit. The future reposes in the keeping of the Almighty. Your anxious mood and vexatious temper will never help to disentangle the mystery. When the morrow comes you may have clearer vision, or the way will open with distinctness or the situation will be entirely changed. Like the Christians in the besieged city of Leyden, you may waken to find your enemies fled and the coast full clear. Or your strength may multiply for the emergency, and reinforcements join you. You may sail out upon a smooth sea when the night promised a storm. You may find that a good pilot stands at the wheel, and if the storm comes his firm hands guide you safely through the trackless waters. The sea may suddenly calm and all journeyings prove untroubled. You may repeat the old experience of Mary and her companions at the tomb of Christ : " They came unto the grave." "They said among themselves, who shall roll us away the stone from the door of the sepulchre ? And when they looked they saw that

the stone *was* rolled away (for it was very great.)"
The task had been done for them. They had only
to enter the tomb.

Friends, the cares of life are many, and they have
peculiar virtue as they train us into work, duty,
service. But they were never distributed to drive
smiles from the face, or to push goodness from the
heart, or to expel blessed hope from the life. "Be
not anxious."

> "Do thy duty, that is best,
> Leave unto the Lord the rest."

WORRY.

WORRY.

" Let me not see my wretchedness."—Numbers x : 15.

"And the Lord said unto Moses, is the Lord's hand waxed short?"—Numbers x : 23.

This prophet Moses seems kinned to the whole world. He passes through dark hours, somber moods, misery experiences, just like the rest of us. It is almost pitiable to think of it. Moses ought to show himself a man unmoved by the common things of life. Has he not fellowshipped with God in close and marvellous way? Has he not been elected to a work of magnificent proportions and illimitable consequences? Has he not been endowed with unique powers and taken the noble part of law writer for a people? Surely such a man ought not to yield to the pressure of petty trials and paltry complainings. But that is the very thing that this brave prophet did. He was sensitive to the worry of life. He illustrates the greatness and littleness of eminent men in his own peculiar fashion. "Let me not see my wretchedness," he exclaims to God, which, being turned into current phrase means, "I am worried to death." Moses had served the Hebrew brethren with singular fidelity and he had chosen "rather to suffer affliction with the people of God, than to enjoy the pleasures of sin for a season." "By faith he forsook Egypt, not fearing the wrath of the king ; for he endured as seeing him who is invisible." But the people fretted. They nour- ished their discontent. They gave way to unreason. "And when the people complained it displeased God." It was not that they did not have *enough* to eat and drink and wear. It was the *kind* of supply that irked them. They wanted better living. Al- though it was a strange journey which they were making, although the circumstances of the case were peculiar, they were dissatisfied and rebellious. The special matter that induced the assault on Moses as recorded in the chapter, was a longing for flesh food. So they assailed Moses with bitter com- plaining. It was not a vital matter. They could live quite comfortably on their present diet. But that did not serve their taste satisfactorily. They demanded another bill of fare. So when Moses went among the people and heard them cry like peevish children, he acted according to impulse, yielded to the vexation of the day, called on God to kill him so that he might evade the wretchedness that dominated his life. He did what history stamps as the popular thing to do : he worried. And his worry took the shape of an appeal to death. " Let me not see my wretchedness." With what patience, affection, wisdom, did God give answer to his querulous prayer. "And the Lord said unto Moses, is the Lord's hand waxed short ?" And in the strength of this fresh revelation the prophet went forth to do the divine bidding.

We propose to point our inquisitiveness worryward. We want to inquire concerning the cause, the
course, the cure of worry. And this incident in the
career of Moses affords us the desired vantage
ground.

We put so much of worry into our life that
definition is superfluous. It is a mental activity
that generally confines itself to things small, dis-
agreeable, uncertain or imaginary, as these things
are supposed to bear upon one's future course and
experience. Temperament has a hand in the thing.
Some favored people are endowed with wonderful
elasticity of nature. They cannot live sad lives.
They are always shining. There seems such an
adjustment of parts and qualities that nothing
comes to the surface but genial words and blithe
activities. But these natures are exceptional. The
majority of people must look to something besides
temperament if they make the days bright with
good cheer. The swiftness of the times has intensified the pressure that bears upon the individual.
This pressure acts energetically upon the temperament. Morbid conditions are easily and speedily
induced. Heredity becomes an important factor.
We meet many people who sing the psalm of life
in a dolorous minor key. And it is a psalm that
gives little refreshment to the listening company,
however much of warning and instruction it may
distribute. Ill health may lend a hand. The nerves
get out of order. Some member, some long-suffer-

ing member of the physical system has a heated controversy with the other members. They get into a jangle and refuse to co-operate. The king cannot tarry unmoved in his palace while his people are waging internecine strife. He is related in such close way to the subjects of his kingdom that their strife has vital significance for him. The man that rules the petty sovereignty of the human frame cannot remain unmoved while one and another member yields to any kind of base or harmful activity. Such condition of forces serves to throw him off his balance, to undermine his mastery of self, to harass and hamper him in any happy living.

Then circumstances have a share in worry. Some people are placed in life so that the years move along with the calm and the monotony of a great sluggish river. The storm does not seem to touch them. They have all the things that heart can desire. But such people can be reckoned on one's fingers. We deceive ourselves concerning them. Circumstances touch all men with vexatious touch. It is a matter of concealment in many cases. And yet it is true that while one life seems quite free from worrisome circumstances another life has superabundance. The mother who lives long days amid her large family of little children, finds herself the creature of worry, how many, many hours. The children fret, the children quarrel, they fall, they tear their clothes, they lose their playthings, they cultivate mischievous pranks, they get ill and cross, and disobedient. What a record of trivialities ! And how easily we can bear them at a distance and in some other family. But when it comes to one's own home, when the trifles multiply into a stormy host ; well it's not such a small matter and unimportant matter after all. These things worry a person. "Oh, that I had wings like a dove, for then would I fly away and be at rest." The psalmist had his hours of worry, and his words voice the cry of many a worn, wearied soul. Yes, circumstances have a great deal to do with the thing. They press the mind into an oversensitive state, and then they make occasion for the final demonstration. Moses bore up with robust courage and triumphant faith so long as the course of Israel was obstructed by the hatred and cruelty of Pharaoh, by the rough waters of the Red Sea, by the grim desolation of the Wilderness ; but when it came to the pettish whimper of the people, when it came to a small matter of variegated diet, he succumbed. " Let me not see my wretchedness." He wanted to die because the people worried him. The circumstance was too much for his equilibrium. Now, when we yield to these things the result is inevitable. We give a very sombre interpretation to life. We form a habit of fret, and a good deal of our thought, experience, vision, finds explanation in this chronic state of soul. Every little annoyance is magnified into importance. It is just like the work which a certain

tiny parasite did for one of the ships of Columbus
when he coasted along the new land of Veragua.
The parasite bored into the thick, tough hide of the
ship until it was as porous as a piece of sponge, and
the ship sank, a worthless wreck, to the bottom of the
sea.   And these petty perplexities attach themselves to the soul and pierce it through and through
until it seems like a worthless wreck of its former
self ; and then how many times there is sad collapse
and inevitable ruin !   It is a miserable kind of life
which one lives who never basks in the sunshine.
It was a mournful day when the Aztec prisoners were
drawn down into the mines and there compelled
to delve in the shadows and darkness.   It meant
loss of strength and premature decrepitude and
joyless living.   And worry means the shutting out
of sunshine.   It means a mournful tarrying in the
shadows.   It means condemnation to dull, weary,
bodeful living.   It means forfeiture of strength and
vitiation of character.   " Let me not see my wretchedness."   So fretted Moses cries and turns toward
the grave as toward a great and blessed relief.   " I
am worried to death," so our tried, vexed spirit cries,
and we reach forth for the same relief that makes
suggestion of its solacement.

But we have had enough of this life condition.
And the Lord said unto Moses, " Is the Lord's hand
waxed short ?" and that is saying that commends
itself to you and to me when we feel the pressure
of worry.   We observe then that life at the best has

a great deal in it that is adapted for purposes of worry. And there are some people who find morbid satisfaction in this fact. They borrow trouble and they beg trouble, that they may worry over it. "Ah," says Mrs. Parrott, who was conscious of her inferiority in this respect, "there isn't many families as have had so many deaths as yours, Mrs. Higgins." It is a sorry prospect for a soul when the drift of daily experience is worryward. Temperament, health, circumstances, they all favor the condition, but God calls a halt upon the soul. "Is the Lord's hand waxed short?" Does your worry make any difference with event or transaction? Is not God master of life, and does He not hold in thought the infinite details of your career? This does not signify that our difficulties and harrassments which multiply day by day, are to be removed and avoided. The divine plan *sometimes* reveals itself in this way, but generally the divine plan takes the shape of obligation on your part, to meet the trial and vexation and resolutely control it. Temperament and health and circumstance are largely under our management. Some of the greatest scholars that the world has ever known were men who had little natural aptitude for such pursuits. They longed for knowledge, but it was tedious, serious labor for them to acquire it. They mastered their defects, and their mastery gave its fruitage in the corresponding achievement. Some of the cheerfulest men that you find in the world have been men of gloomy tem-

per and morbid tendency. They were compelled to
put all effort, determination, skill, into just this
simple conquest of natural inclination, and they
gained as their guerdon a sunniness and hopefulness of character that testify to a very precious fellowship with God.   We are to face these little things
and press them into serviceableness.   We are to
make account of them.   The old saw has it that you
take care of the pennies and the pounds will take
care of themselves.   When we put the teaching into
spiritual terms it means that you prove watchful
and obedient concerning the petty and the trivial
oppositions, and you will necessarily be drilled into
deft and masterful dealing with large and supreme
matters.   It is the law of faithfulness which, assert-
ing itself in that which is least as a matter of necessity, asserts itself in that which is greatest.

Water is a cruel, relentless master.   When it
rushes through the canyons after the storm has
deluged the mountain, it doesn't tarry upon the
pleasure of the traveler—it doesn't favor him with
anything of kindness.   With swift, strong grasp it
bears him down to death and hurries along its
tumultuous coursings.   But the same force has fine
possibilities.   The water itself may be used for purposes of irrigation—while the force that is concealed
in the swift descending stream may be transferred
into looms and wheels, and manufactured products.
And steam is a harsh and savage master.   When it
bursts forth from its imprisonment it scalds and

ruins, and destroys with indescribable speed and efficiency. But when we lead this force into harness and guide this force with strong bits, steam serves us with a devotedness and a generosity that are unparalleled.

What we call temper—all the things which shape themselves into worry—represent a mighty force. And the forces which show themselves as anxiety and heedful anticipation, *must* be transformed into trust, confidence, resignation, praise. And the Lord said unto Moses, " Is the Lord's hand waxed short ?" The thought or teaching is this : God will stand just as close to us when the petty trial comes as when the great trial approaches us. And experience emphasizes the need just as sternly on the one occasion as on the other. The fact of worry is largely explained in a serious neglect of God's help. Like proud, conceited children, we propose to "shift for ourselves" in the small concerns. When some great need presses us we will take counsel with God and draw upon Him for help. But counsel is just as much a necessity in the one case as in the other : and help has its part to play with both experiences. It is only a difference of degree. The same kind of raw material is used in making the small diamond as in making the Kohinoor. It requires a larger amount of the raw material to make the Kohinoor—that is the thing that differences it from the pure small gems that glitter upon our fingers. It requires the same kind of raw

D

material to make a small noble deed as it does a
large noble deed. It requires the same kind of
gracious resistance to convert a petty temptation
into a soul victory as it does to shape the mighty
onset into a soul victory. It is a matter of degree,
and the Lord's hand is not shortened, that He will
refuse you if you ask for help when you are enticed
into trivial meannesses and worrisome activities as
well as when you meet the heavier attacks of great
troubles. The truth that Scripture tries to put into
the mind is this : that the Lord is a very present
Help and there is no limitation touching the precise
size and relative importance of the various troubles
incident to our life. "My grace is sufficient for
thee." I take it that Christ meant we could learn
to bear ourselves with serenity and hopefulness
during the moment of trifling insult and personal
pique as well as during the hour of heavy bereave-
ment and sorrowful defeat.

We make another advance when we consider that
the Master works with design through the little
troubles as well as through the great ones. When
some marked change has been wrought in our life
by events that were important, and when we have
earnestly endeavored to adjust ourselves to these
events and the issue has proved significant, we
believe that God was guiding and determining for
us. We rest in his providence. Infinite comfort
possesses our soul. But God wants to use the small
occurrences of life and the unimportant trials for

the same purpose. Every leaf bears relation to the perfected rose. Every experience bears relation to the perfected spirit. Nothing comes amiss in life so long as we give God free activity in our living. It is when we rebel or play truant or refuse to heed, that things go amiss. The jangle of personal life reverts to disobedience and carelessness and unbelief. The thing that frets a person must be used as a thing that urges him into such gracious opposition that the person will *not* fret. The thing that wears the person into roughness of temper is the very thing that he must use with God's help in the training of his temper, so that he shall be calm and Christ-like.

This leads to the final statement. It is the petty affair, the small trial, the insignificant friction of life, that does the *fine* work of character making. Fine qualities require fine tools. Raphael cannot paint the Transfiguration with a great coarse brush and Phidais cannot carve his goddess with a massive chisel. Fine work demands fine instruments. The large mallet and the broad chisel take away the masses of stone; but the small instruments are essential to the delicate task. These things of life that make men worry are the small tools that bear down upon the manhood and the womanhood with keenest persistency. They are doing the fine work for the soul. Great deeds and conspicuous labors bring into prominence the great traits of character. Trivial deeds and inconspicuous victories witness

to a matchless refinement and. beauteousness of
character. God would use the crooked impulse and
vexatious motive, and all the things that urge us
into worry, just as the artist uses tiny bristles and
neutral tints. These are the agencies which work
grace and fineness in the spirit.

The cathedral of Cologne has its small, obscure
parts wrought into the same beauty and perfectness
as the large and dominant features of the structure.
It signifies a thoroughness, an exquisiteness of finish
that is rich in precious suggestion. And that is the
way God tries to deal with us. He plans to work us
into that shapeliness of soul which is described in
Jesus Christ. We are to take the forces of worry
and give God opportunity to use them in the making
of our character. He will work in us and through
us. And this illustrates the divine method of teaching the world and exalting the spirit.

TRIBULATION.

TRIBULATION.

"In the world ye have tribulation."—John xvi : 33.

That is a fact. The saying is one whose truth is so patent that we can afford to omit the proof. "In the world ye have tribulation." It is written in furrowed faces, in bent forms, in sunken eyes, in silvered locks. It is chanted in the monotonous minor of sickness, decay, separation, death. It is proclaimed in tragic tone and gesture by calamity, distress, iniquity, crime. "In the world *ye* have tribulation." In respect to other people, unbelieving people, godless people, we call it by another name, for it is another thing. *Ye*, the souls that fellow-ship with Christ, have tribulation. And you have it because you need it. You have it because with the present order of things you could not get along without it. Just how we are to interpret tribulation is the object of our inquiry.

The word comes from the Latin *tribulum*, which means a roller, the threshing instrument of the Roman husbandman. Tribulation signifies an act of separation—a threshing. When Christianized the word came to have a nobler meaning, even "the separating in man of whatever in him was light, trivial and poor from the solid and the true,"—the threshing of the spiritual man. So tribulation evolves a meaning that makes it synonymous with anguish, affliction, sorrow. And the part that these factors take in human life on earth affords us opportunity to observe the means of moral growth and development.

There is a great deal in human nature that must be threshed out of it. Tribulation is a process of coercion. It is help in the line of fruitful harvests if one can keep the weeds under firm control. A thrifty vice will sap all the vitality that is required to make a robust virtue. Some people put so much strength into self-conceit, that they show little vigor in practical industry or serious application. Tribulation takes them in hand. How are the mighty fallen! One lively hour of thorough threshing will sometimes do more for a soul than long years of subtle argument and importunate entreaty. An infidel miner, proud in his own conceit, was tugging away at his task in an English mine. Suddenly one of the kobs of coal crashed down the shaft and felled the poor miner to the floor. But he was conscious of his hurt and his peril, and so he cried with great fury of zeal, "God have mercy on me." One of his comrades, a devout soul, was quick to appreciate the situation. "Ah," said he, "there's nothing like kobs of coal for knocking the infidelity out of a man." Tribulation in the shape of kobs of coal, or shipwreck, or painful illness, threshes many a soul so that life has nobler meaning and richer promise.

What variety of tendencies manifest themselves in the heart of your child. And you must discriminate between the good and the bad. And then you must work to repress the bad and foster the good. The tribulations of childhood are real and rough, severe and taxing. But we now see the blessedness of them. How many times did our parents punish us for disobediences—those rebellious tendencies of our heart were powerful—they sometimes attained the mastery. But the tribulations ordained by our loving guardians did some precious work of restraint and correction, and we can see that there was a certain winnowing in our life that issued in a purer and stronger personality. This is parallel with the way of God. When we outgrow the garments of childhood we still find our souls so small that they have to wear clothes of about the same size. God is obliged to treat us in very much the same way as we, through love, are obliged to treat our children. Our soul growth doesn't keep pace with our body growth. So we have tribulation in the world.

We know well that when people make effort to live clean, Christian lives they are subjected to the assaults of what is termed the world—ungodly society. You cannot serve two masters. Light and darkness cannot abide each other's company. There is no friendship between righteousness and iniquity. So we can truthfully say that tribulation (as we apply the word to Christ's people) means service in the employ of virtue. It tests a man's honesty and genuineness. The early church was greatly blessed in persecution. Dishonest and insincere men were driven from its shelter. And troubles operate in the same way. They make a man show his metal. One will throw off his mask if it has got him into peril. The natural man will assert himself with all speed and strength. In this way tribulation sometimes determines the quality of a man's faith. If I am not comforted, supported, encouraged as I suffer, it seems a correct conclusion that my faith is not of the finest quality. Tribulation is strenuous in its faith requirements. "Though I walk through the valley of the shadow of death, I will fear no evil." That is the saying of sterling faith. So tribulation sometimes leads us down into the shadowy valley for the very purpose of putting test to this condition of heart. If we be genuine in our life—if we prove true to our professions— such experiences serve to strengthen the spiritual stamina. Tribulation inducts one into nobler living. Life is broadened, deepened, solidified, intensified by such operations. This seems to be the meaning of those words in Acts xiv: 22, "We must through much tribulation enter into the kingdom of heaven." Our whole earth life, we see, is given over to moral tests. The spirit is to be tutored into patience, long-suffering, kindness, charity, gentleness, hope by the sombre work of tribulation.

But if we look at this matter from another point of view we shall find a larger significance in it. Tribulation is a thorough, persistent, sagacious and accomplished instructor. Shakespeare says that all the world's a stage and we are actors on it : and that sounds well. But all the world's a school and we are pupils in it. Trouble is one of the teachers. The majority of people are dull when it comes to the realm of morals. They read the law, they recite with variations the precepts that grow out of the moral law : and then they go like wilful children and do as they please. It isn't enough for such people, for most people, that they receive oral or written instructions concerning these things. So God has made this world school on the kindergarten plan. Object teaching has been in vogue since Adam and Eve were driven from the Garden of Eden—indeed before that sad expulsion—for Satan himself made use of this admirable system when he taught two people the knowledge of good and evil, by the use of an apple.

You remember how Paul says, "we glory in tribulation." That is a proper thing to say. We glory in a fine teacher. The having such a teacher, is an earnest of good attainments and thorough culture. "I am exceeding joyful in all our tribulations," writes the apostle, and one does not eye the words dubiously when one observes that the schooling which a man gets while studying under tribulation has in it such potency of things good and true.

The great Teacher looks down into our life and finds that we are intensely selfish. Now there is only one convenient way to get that selfishness out of the heart. The Master says, "I will put this heart under the schooling of tribulation." So this subordinate teacher begins the task. The man loses some measure of his prosperity. He is prostrated upon a bed of illness. He is thrust out of his conspicuous position. He sees his adored child pine away with disease. His heart is almost broken with trouble. He passes through various states of anger, bitterness, despair. Then he pays some heed to the voices that whisper to his soul. He begins to think that he is not of great importance to the world—that the things of life move along with method and regularity without even his touch or impulse—that it is not the chief end of living—this having everybody minister to him. The man finds under the serious, persevering instructions of tribulation that he is a mean, selfish person, and that such meanness and selfishness are hateful in sight of men and accursed in sight of God. It teaches in matter-of-fact way, with such repetition of the lesson, with such reiterated illustration of the lesson, that one cannot evade or escape for long, the assigned task. No doubt many of us tarry under such instructions needlessly. Like restive, inattentive little pupils, we refuse to learn, and so the teacher keeps us in the school and we drag out weary hours of rebellious study. " In the world ye have tribulation.". But the instructions of this teacher are not given in any haphazard way. There is what might be called a curriculum of troubles. We are taking a full course. The petty trials of childhood, the vexations of youth, the reverses of manhood, the disappointments of maturity, the infirmities of age, and running all through these experiences, the incidental griefs, pains, calamities, these make up the curriculum of the tribulation School. You see that the great Father is training us for a career. That is why you send your songful child to the conservatory of Milan, you are training her for a career. There are marvellous possibilities in her voice. So you bind her down to humdrum, burdensome living. She keeps her voice in perpetual exercise ; she studies the masters ; she has all the imperfections and infirmities threshed out of her, (so far as the Milan conservatory can do such threshing.) This is teaching in another sphere or realm. And it pays. Your child, now a mature woman, begins her career. You sit in the great hall—one heart in the midst of thousands—and you hear the song that is interpreted by your child's voice. Its sweetness, pathos, compass, power, thrill every heart and move the multitude with nameless emotion. In joy, in worth, and in work, it has paid. And so the great Father is training us for a career. He sends us to the appointed school. "Oh what powers lie hidden in these souls," he says, "I must prepare them for a great career." In the world ye have tribulation. Living seems burdensome, sometimes; this constant exercise of small, weak graces, the ceaseless struggle with infirmities and imperfections, the earnest counsel of daily troubles—but it pays—this tribulation pays. It is preparing us for a great career; the hidden powers shall reveal themselves; the songful spirit shall in the end make its exquisite music. You have seen during the years of your training, some brave, tranquil men whose lives were beautifully melodious. They were saints who had been graduated from the School of tribulation. They were waiting to begin the new career in that larger life-named heaven.

Bearing these definitions in mind, we observe that tribulation is one of the necessary factors in the perfect unfolding of the man. It will do for the growing personality what the rough storm will do for the growing plant and tree—refresh, invigorate, strengthen, nourish. People make great mistakes in respect to the object of living. The gratification of appetite, the free play of ambition, the pursuit of happiness—these are the things that deceive us. And these things reduce life to an experience of petty, sterile selfishness. Tribulation comes to set things "to rights." "Whom the Lord loveth He chasteneth." Love never permits her children to have their own reckless, wilful way through the world. The thorn in the flesh is decreed so that you shall be brought to your senses.

There is no malice or hatred in such visitation. Tribulation keeps saying to men, the primary object of living is not simple enjoyment of the world. There are large measures of legitimate pleasure and felicity in this variegated world career, but these things are secondary. We are put into the world to use it. It is like a great store house of tools and instruments. We are to learn the various uses of things, to practice certain activities, and so work out our own salvation. We are to equip ourselves for the exercises of the other world, and tribulation serves persistently in the way of soul equipment.

It makes infinite difference whether we take a short view or a long view of life. If our days are simply seventy years and all ends, we must bustle about our little court, trying to make the most of our transient living. But tribulation bids us take the long view of life. We tarry here for brief season that we may fit ourselves for the endless career. We gain here what heaven itself cannot give us—a tried, toughened, personal worth.

Alfieri in Ferrara looking at the precious MSS. of Ariosto, checked with innumerable corrections, evidencing the writer's industry, wrote "Alfieri beholds and venerates." We observe the faithful, forceful way in which tribulation does its noble task in the lives of Christian men. We also say "we behold and venerate." But there is a richer saying, which I urge you to use as voicing a nobler

sentiment : "We also glory in tribulation, knowing
that tribulation worketh patience ; patience, experience, and experience, hope ; and hope maketh not
ashamed."

SUFFERING.

E

SUFFERING.

"For this is thankworthy, if a man for conscience toward God endure grief, suffering wrongfully. For what glory is it, if, when ye be buffeted for your faults, ye shall take it patiently? but if, when ye do well, and suffer for it, ye take it patiently, this is acceptable with God."—I. Pet. ii : 19 and 20.

Sometimes a precious truth will express itself in the life of a man and the man fails to measure its importance and meaning. Just as sunshine uses air as a medium of service, so the truthshine may use the unconscious man. But the things that touch us with supreme touch generally are the things that come to us through personal interpretation and through personal illustration. All talk about divine love is vague and indistinct until we meet love in Jesus Christ. God so loved the world that He gave His son. The cross becomes the everlasting symbol of the God love ; and when we name many subordinate truths, it is only when we meet them incarnated that their worthiness and their beauty and their glory are emphasized. A saying multiplies its significance many fold when it is uttered under the impulse of deep personal knowledge. This explains in some measure the roughness and perilousness of the Apostles' journeyings. Any healthful, inspiring, convictive statement concerning spiritual matters, necessitated some notable share in such experience as was to be phrased into a truth statement. Truth is truth. But there seems to be the demand on the part of this poor human nature, that truth must have a *man* behind it to give it its mighty forcefulness and make it do its great ordained mission. So when one man says a thing we make little account of it. But when some other man says the same thing we make large account of it. It is the personal factor that sends the truth home to the soul. The Bible deals in deeds and men. It does not run its teaching into abstract forms to any large degree. It seeks to make its instruction concrete. It folds lesson after lesson within the personality of Moses, David, Judas, Felix, Peter and the host of Bible men and women. As we listen to these men we observe that they communicate truth through the life they live—we observe that revelation itself is so tinged and toned by the inspired writers that it is a matter of endless discussion to discriminate the human from the divine. But what difference does it make to the learner so long as he seeks the truth and finds the truth and lives the truth?

Now, the narrative of Peter's life is brightened and darkened by an experience that was singularly varied. The counsel which he pushes into our heart in these text words, is counsel and comfort whose merit had been tested in his own career. He could talk therefore with directness and precision. It does not count much for a man

who is rich and strong and prosperous to say to
the poor man who languishes in illness and penury,
"Now be serene and contented, dear man. Don't
worry or complain. This is your lot. God knows
best." Such language does not carry a very large
burden of comfort and helpfulness. It is when a
man puts himself into sympathy with the sufferer
—it is when the man suffers with the sufferer, (by
sacrifice or kindred experience,) that such messages
carry helpfulness and solacement. Now these words
of our text had a man behind them. He knew the
significance of his message. It was braced and
shaped and vitalized by Peter's personality. The
truth was lively with the robust manhood of Peter.
You hold this doctrine of dutiful submission in
great honor as you see it lived by a man of impetu-
ous spirit, zealous nature, indomitable will, un-
quenchable hope. It is this sort of a man, (not a
weak, dubious, effeminate, coward creature,) who
insists that "it is thankworthy, if a man for conscience toward God endure grief, suffering wrongfully. For what glory is it, if, when ye be buffeted
for your faults, ye shall take it patiently? but if, when
ye do well, and suffer for it, ye take it patiently,
this is acceptable with God."

In these words Peter tells us what should be the
attitude of the soul toward men who harass
and trammel the man in his daily service. Its
primary application was made to that class of
people who were subject to the bondage of earthly

masters. But its secondary application touches
any heart that tries to do right in the world
and meets censure, opposition, scorn in such
doing. You see then that Peter has good help for
us. He seeks to arm us with grace against the inevitable conflicts that are incident to every godly
life that shall be lived on earth. It isn't any virtue
to take a scourging gracefully when we deserve it.
The scourging evidences our lack of virtue. And
yet it isn't every man who merits punishment that
does take it resignedly. The majority of us manifest a purpose to whine or kick, or take vengeance.
Now, says Peter, (and Peter simply varies the
Christ exposition on this point,) this is not only
mean and unchristian, but our keeping still and
taking chastisement isn't a thing worth praising.

There is no virtue in such a line of conduct. It
is when ye do *well* and suffer for it and take it
patiently that you show an acceptable spirit to God.
"For even hereunto were ye called," continues
Peter ; "because Christ also suffered for us, leaving
us an example, that ye should follow his steps ; who
did no sin, neither was guile found in his mouth :
who, when he was reviled, reviled not again ; when
he suffered, he threatened not ; but committed himself to Him that judgeth righteously." O Thou Son
of God, despised and rejected of men ; a man of
sorrows and acquainted with grief ; Thou who wast
wounded for our transgressions and bruised for our
iniquities ; impart unto us Thine own kingly spirit,
that we may endure as seeing Him who is invisible!

To do well and suffer for it, and then to take the suffering patiently, that is acceptable to God. There are three phases to the experience that is outlined in Peter's words. First comes the well-doing. There must be no uncertainty in respect to that matter. It will prove vain to pursue a course of self-deception and try to make one's self think that ill-doing is well-doing. It is not enough to say that " happy is that man which condemneth not him-self in that which he alloweth." The thing is put in positive, definite form. It is well-doing as measured by the thought of God. Pseudo-martyr-dom does not count. It is the genuine spirit of good, true work that is signified by the phrase.

The second phase of the experience is suffering for righteous conduct. So long as we hold acquaint-anceship with the world, the flesh and the Devil, we shall find steady business in the shape of trouble. All the harassments and conflicts of life do not come as penalty for our disobedience or rebellion. A true man is frequent vicar. To accomplish any-thing large and valuable in behalf of men, we are compelled to invest considerable soul. That means suffering, sacrifice, opposition, disturbance. We must learn that such thing is part of the price which we pay for the spiritual achievement. And when we learn this fact we grasp with firm hand the third phase of the experience—the patience of the thing. It is a part of the divine thought that we suffer patiently. Jesus held that attitude toward persecution. And the disciple is not above his Master. When we put our share of work into clear, accurate terms, we shall see that patient endurance is a frequent term with manifold relations.

All of which exposition words lead us to inquire wherein consists the acceptableness of such course to God. "To do well and suffer for it and take it patiently, is acceptable with God." This is pointing in the direction of spiritual enlargement. How easily the words which state this teaching flow from our lips! But it is not such an easy matter to explain these words through personal dealing.

The acceptableness of this spirit is seen in the fact that it signifies a training into forbearance. Practicing this text is a kind of message to God that we are marching along the line of personal conquest. When the child has mastered his task he receives good impulse for the coming hour. His nature acts under the healthful stimulation of success. He is well toned for further effort. So the soul that learns to take pain patiently—the pain that comes from rough encounters in behalf of right—is learning to look with generous forbearance upon the faults and infirmities of our fellow-men. The noble attitude for the soul to take when assaulted by the world, is illustrated by our Saviour. Even when the rabble taunted Him as He wore away the anguishful hours upon the cross, He spake with infinite tone of acquiescence and compassion, "Father, forgive them, for they know not what they do." This is molding the lower nature into such form that it shall fit the higher nature and give it the noblest interpretation. This is putting to shame the base tendencies of the heart and impressing their force into the service of God.

The acceptableness of this soul attitude is seen in the fact that it develops a peculiar courage. It sometimes requires more strength to refrain from doing a thing than is required for the doing of the thing. Washington founding the Republic is not so great as Washington declining the royal crown. The greatness of men is often tested by their not doing, and the courage which enables a man to say no and remain quiet when his wishes, and his passions, and his comrades urge him to say yes and push him into doing, is courage of finer quality and larger merit than courage which issues in world conquest. That is a fine sentiment which we read in Prov. xvi: 32. "He that is slow to anger is better than the mighty : and he that ruleth his spirit than he that taketh a city." And it makes unforgetable impression when illustrated in Christian character. The courage that is turned towards one's self and made to resist pride, hatred, viciousness, madness, is courage of superb type—courage that stamps the soul as vigorous servant of God. That is the kind of courage fostered by our text. If you want to know its merit and beauty apply it to the affairs of life that demand forbearance, magnanimity, forgiveness.

The acceptableness of this attitude of the soul is
seen in the fact that it encourages faith. We are in-
structed with marked particularity in the Bible that
"vengeance is mine, I will repay saith the Lord."
That is instruction that does not suit the pugnacious
spirit of the natural man. We insist on present con-
dign punishment, and as the sure way of enforcing
such punishment we form a kind of lynch-law habit
and take the administration of justice into our own
hands. We understand this matter thoroughly
when we take the trouble to investigate. The fact
is we are trying to do God's business on our own responsibility and in our own chosen way. When
God wants us to punish men for the injuries which
they have inflicted upon us, He will put us in law-
ful position for the task and give us legitimate
weapons to inflict the chastisement. But we are
blind with passion and we fear the escape of the
culprit, and so we break the law ourselves and vent
the strength of our madness upon the offender. As
if God did not see men ; as if God did not measure
every transaction ; as if God did not have supreme
control of all agencies and activities ; as if God did
not purpose a discreet course and shape His provi-
dences with infinite wisdom. "Oh, ye of little
faith." It is a discipline of faith—this living the
teaching framed in our text. It is a masterful
method of courting faith into bud, and bloom, and
fruitage. Take God at His word. Leave the matter
of castigation to Him. Do well and suffer for it,

and bear it patiently, and bide the time of the Omnipotent. Faith pushes its way into the sunshine ; the years bring the testimonies as to right or wrong. Faith bursts into precious blossom ; the years continue their work of sifting. Faith yields its perfect fruitage. The years finish the task of of righteous judgment. The spirit of the text cherishes a faith that waxes stronger and stronger until we learn personally to leave all complex, puzzling things, all dark, inexplicable occurrences to the decision and adjustment of the great Father.

The acceptableness of this attitude of the soul is seen in the fact that it takes us along the way that ends in subjection to God. A man begins to feel his ignorance, weakness, insignificance, simpleness. He wants to subject himself to a leader that is strong, wise, righteous, divine. Self-mastery and Christ-mastery run into the same channel. " When I am weak then am I strong." That paradox expresses a condition of soul that has infinite potency. As we put ourselves under the leadership of Jesus, as we obey His words, and reveal His mind, and do His works, and share His spirit, we grow away from annoyance, anxiety, hatred, wrong. To do well and suffer for it and bear the suffering patiently, is most precious training into God subjection. The very force of soul that is put into the denial and restraint, is force of soul that wins the Master's support, and solace. " The Lord reigns." Mark that everlasting message ! It is vain for men to meddle with the plans and tasks of God. When the Master wants our help, when the Master requires our agency, He will voice His will, not through our passions and impulses, but through conscience, reason, circumstance, instruction.

We see then that the method recommended by this text constrains the soul into greatness. This is acceptable with God that a man pursue such course and phrase such conduct, that he shall rise into moral greatness. We cannot dictate the terms of our living. We cannot push vice, crime, sin, out of the world. It is not for us to pronounce upon many things that wear us and afflict us, and scourge us. But this we learn, that any thought or feeling of bitterness, hatred, cursing, malice, vengeance, will vitiate the soul and darken the years. No man can afford to harbor aught against his fellows. The injury reverts to one's self. To do well and suffer for it, and bear it patiently, that is acceptable with God. It is acceptable with God because it is Christ-like. It marks the Master's way of dealing with men. It leaves judgment and penalty with the All-Wise. But it is acceptable with God for another reason. It leads the soul into forbearance, courage, faith, submission, and so gives God a precious harvest in the autumn of our years.

Friends, " do well ; and if you suffer for it, bear it patiently ; for this is acceptable with God." May this noble doctrine push its way into your life ! May it impart virtue to your career of trial ! And

may the God of love sanctify the things of daily
experience, to the end that you attain the symmetry
of perfect Christian manhood.

DISCIPLINE.

DISCIPLINE.

"I pray not that thou shouldest take them out of the world, but that thou shouldest keep them from the evil."—John xvii: 15.

This intercessory prayer of Christ was the favorite reading of John Knox. It has proved sweetest and most nourishing pasturage to the great flock of the Good Shepherd. The verse which we choose for our study centers its immediate significance in the apostles. "I pray not that thou shouldest take them out of the world, but that thou shouldest keep them from the evil." The work of founding the church was to make its beginnings at the hands of these same apostles. This work required their personal ministry. They could not do it were they taken with Christ into the heaven land; neither could they do it were they retired into the desert in the role of recluse or ascetic. Christ therefore supplicates the Father that He fit them for such service; that He train them into the destined career; that He encompass them with safeguards, and when the Master has proceeded in his prayer he enlarges his petitions so that they gather into their meaning all that believe upon His name. "Neither pray I for these alone, but for them also which shall believe on me through their word." The ultimate sweep of the prayer includes the illimitable company of Christian men and women.

F

Now, this prayer teaches us many precious truths concerning the divine procedure. The great truth that is voiced by our text has to do with certain phases of discipline. "I pray not that thou shouldest take them out of the world, but that thou shouldest keep them from the evil" (of the world).

We naturally suppose that if any prayer ever receives full triumphant answer it will be the prayer of Jesus. For we are sure that his prayer parallels the will of God, and that is equivalent to saying that it will be transacted to the very letter. So we begin our study with the serene assurance that when we measure the meaning of Christ's petition, we shall face the rich and satisfactory response. The world, as the Master uses the word, stands for this present, narrow, trammeled, checkered relation. It isn't nature that is signified; it isn't mind that is signified. But it is nature and mind as they are related to a heart condition. "The heart is deceitful above all things and desperately wicked." The self-determination of man has revealed itself in changes which issue in disturbance, separation, ruin. Matter and mind are touched with the curse of sin. The world means that time realm which is conditioned by this particular part of creation and that particular lapse from virtue, and Christ does not propose that we be taken prematurely from out this environment of fret, battle, sin, wickedness.

You will observe that a good many of our prayers run contrary to this petition of Christ. We often ask with no small vehemence of spirit that God shall remove us from present surroundings, or that he shall dispense with our present surroundings. It does not seem to us that we can bear the things that are desolating our life and stealing our comfort and happiness. So we pray that God may literally take us out of the world. "I want to die," "I want to die," and the cry is wrung from our soul by the bitterness and agony of our affliction. Or we pray that God may, as it *were*, take us out of the world, remove us to more congenial and inspiring associations, crush the forms and individuals and activities that antagonize our soul. That is human nature—unsanctified human nature. It just thinks of self, prays for self and orders for self, and in thought gives God's plan and the right plan the "go-by" in so far as such a thing is possible. Christ teaches us the folly and the futility of such petition.

Our doctrine of prayer needs radical change. It is grounded in error, the doctrine of prayer which many of us hold; it is fostered by misconceptions, and we get very small comfort and encouragement through such prayer. The asking of favors is the prevalent interpretation of prayer. So when a man gets into what he calls a tight place he prays. I knew two boys who were overtaken by a storm as they fished on the broad bay. They were two miles from shore. Their little

boat was like a cockle shell when the winds and
waves beat furiously against them.   In their zeal
and terror they broke one oar and the other was
snatched from their grasp by a great, boisterous
wave.   And then it seemed all vain.   They thought
they were lost.   But there was a last resort.   They
went to praying, and they prayed with such agony
of spirit that their very bodies sweat great drops
of sweat.   Prayer was the last resort.   They were
in direful extremity.   They prayed for rescue.
Well, they *were* rescued.   They are living to-day,
and I doubt if they have made any great advance
in their conceptions of the privilege and office of
prayer.   How different the spirit of a famous Christian woman who was traveling down the Rhine when
the boat was suddenly beset by a storm.   It did not
seem possible that they could out-ride the treacher-
ous gale, and she prayed.   But it wasn't any selfish
petition for mere life.   Her face shone with faith,
peace, love, hope.   She calmed her associate pas-
sengers.   Her prayer was vital with assurance.
She felt God's presence.   She was not alarmed.
She chose neither life nor death.   She sought simply
the will of her Master.   That was petition phrased
in loyal accord with this prayer of Christ.   It was
conformity to the mind and heart of God that was
pleaded.   The mere texture of externalities and
circumstances was matter of secondary importance.
" I pray not that they may be taken out of the
world."   Their place is *in* the world.   They not only

have a work to do, but they have a life to life. "I pray that thou shouldest keep them from the evil."

This divine system of discipline finds suggestive analogy in our experience with the children. We do not expect to put our children out of harm's way by isolating them from temptation and immuring them in solitary places. They must meet the ills and trials and vices and sorrows that are incident to the world. So we school them into resistance of these things—making some beginning in the very first days of their career. We cannot always have them clinging to us for support. We want them to have a certain independency that is part of manhood. It seems very hard that we are compelled to separate them from us and trust them to the rough usage of men. And they will suffer many things ere they attain that mastery which makes them attractive to men and competent for affairs ; nevertheless it is for their good that we subject them to such discipline. Some of us remember the time when we were compelled to leave the old home and bind us down to the routine of school. I remember such an youth. He was put in preparatory school when he was fifteen years of age. He loved home. He had always been a home boy. But it was time that he fit for college and for life. So he was enrolled with some three hundred pupils, in a great school. Words are poorest kind of pigments when you use them to paint that boy's homesickness. His suffering was terrible. And everybody pitied him. (That may have been one of the worst features of the case.) The boys pitied him; the teachers pitied him; the servants pitied him. He would not eat. He could not study. And I have seen some of the letters that that boy wrote to his parents. What letters! I recall the fact that I advised his parents to burn them. These letters were the most pathetic appeals; and they troubled the parents. But they loved their boy too much to be moved into such an indiscretion as that of yielding to his prayer. They made him stay and defy his homesickness. And it were needless to say that he blessed them a thousand times in later years that they were firm and loyal in their purpose. The boy needed the discipline that carried so much misery with it. It was an essential factor in his success. And the later years revealed the righteousness, the wisdom, the love that insisted upon the course. Now that outlines the Heavenly Father's procedure with His children when they find themselves in very "trying circumstances." He does not want to make them suffer. No parent likes to make a child suffer. In truth the parent sometimes suffers just as much or a good deal more than the child. (And do we not see God in Christ taking to Himself our sins and receiving wounds for our transgressions?) But the parent sees the necessity of discipline and the discipline is decreed. But we people are just like the children. "Don't make me do this thing;

please don't send me to this place ! " That is the
way the child pleads.   And that is the very spirit
of our earnest prayer in the ear of God.   " Don't
compel me to pursue such a course ! Take me away
from this circumstance ! Don't send me here or there!
(as the case may be). I can't stand it ! "   So we dictate to God and beseech Him to modify His plan.
Well, and what comes of it ?   Do you yield to your
short-sighted, untrained child and refrain from the
way indicated by wisdom and affection ?   No ; you
just proceed according to wise system.   You
trust to the years to set the matter right.   And
the child suffers, endures, gets chastisement, and
goes through quite a tangled experience of life.
This is analogous to God's procedure with His
children of a larger growth.   Our place is in
the world.   As things are arranged a man pays
the cost of his manhood in the hard coin of personal resistance and conquest.   It is a tremendous strain upon his little strength and frail
spirit to thread his way through the world and
not swerve to the right or left, and not turn
aside to cull its bright seductive flowers.   And a
great many of us fail to control ourselves and give
the good spirit full opportunity to possess our
hearts and confirm us in the right.   I knew a little
girl who came to visit a neighbor.   A great flower
garden surrounded the old home, and the little girl
had been taught to leave the flowers alone ; they did
not belong to her ; she might look upon them.   But

that was the extent of her legitimate enjoyment.
But one day the child wandered through the
garden alone.   Those flowers were indescribably en-
ticing.   They seemed to say, "pick me! pick! how
beautiful I am! how fragrant!"   And this little girl
yielded to their persuasions.   And when she had
culled a beautiful bouquet the recollection of com-
mands and instructions surged through her soul.
How should she face the mistress and what excuse
could she make?   I saw the child enter the house.
Her face was a curious study ; wrong was there, and
disobedience, and a certain air of deprecation : but
pride, and battle, and determination were there.
She crossed the room with her flowers, showed
them with charming grace to the mistress, and
suavely said : "You see, I have helped myself."
Yes, indeed !   She had helped herself.   And that is
human nature.   And that is the tone and language
of statement as we make explanation to conscience
and to God concerning the lapses and disobediences which result from our disloyalty to the
divine procedure.   The bright things of life as well
as the dark things of life have to be faced.
Every good gift and every perfect gift cometh
down from God.   But a great many things that
have an appearance of pleasure impartation, things
that are wrong, bad, unholy, shameful in themselves, or in their relations, are to be passed un-
touched ; and it may prove just as hard to deny
ourselves these very things as it is grievous and

painful to endure the rougher struggle with trouble, and harassment, and anxiety. " You see I have helped myself." It will not satisfy conscience or God. Whatever may be said as to extenuating circumstances—right is right, and obedience is obedience, and character is character. We are put into the world. Here is the appointed field for our service. This is the disciplinary epoch. There is a noble, individual career. But it touches sorrow, iniquity, affliction, crime, wretchedness, at every point of the course. That is according to the ordainment of the Almighty. " I do not pray that thou shouldest take them out of the world ; I pray that thou shouldest keep them from the evil."

Now, allegiance to this truth signifies infinite succour to the Christian heart.

We might as well quit the making such prayers as dictate in absolute terms the course of God in respect to ourselves. Even our Saviour did not venture upon such unqualified petition. It was his heart and his mind to do God's will. So he submitted to suffering with no thought of evasion. The keenness of his anguish can not be measured. He asked that the cup might pass away if it were God's will. "Nevertheless, not my will but thine be done." And you will observe how these experiences of great agony were followed by the ministry of heaven. After Christ was tempted angels ministered to him. During his Gethsemane trial another heavenly messenger strengthened him. The

bitter cry upon the cross was changed to one of perfect resignation. "Father, into thy hands I commend my spirit." He meets the wickedness and
the sufferingness that belong to the world life.
But He meets these things to the end that He may
conquer them, confirm His soul in its mastery, reveal His character to men, and achieve His sublime
mission.

Friends, the mastership of life is not to be gained
by playing coward and hiding us away from trouble.
You are not taught to pray, that God shall remove
you from trial whether it accords with the divine will
or not. You need not expect to grow into stalwart-
ness and robustness of Christian character by any
desertion from duty, or any flinching under pain, or
any retirement from discipline. "I pray not that
thou shouldest take them out of the world." Neither
are you to make any such prayer. God will take you
out of the world in good time. God will remove
the thorn in the flesh on proper occasion. God will
straighten the tangle of circumstances when He
sees fit. "I pray that thou shouldest keep them
from the evil." *That* is the prayer you need to
make. You are sure as to the rightness, the wisdom, the blessedness of such a course.

How much it all means to us toilsome, disheart-
ened people. Is it possible that these very occa-
sions and experiences which we have thought to
avoid are not only the disciplines that shape us
into nobility, but are also the very means by which

God makes closest approach to our soul and gives sweetest testimony as to the realness of His presence! Is it possible that God employs this rigid system to press us into thought upon Himself, and to urge us into glad assurance of His divine helpfulness! Is it possible that God selects this kind of life apprenticeship with the purpose of courting us into a great, palpitant, victorious, all-ministering sympathy with men?

Man of business, pursue your honorable career seeking that help in trial and gloom which is vouchsafed you. That is your line of prayer and labor. Woman of sorrows, pine not that you are grievously circumstanced. "Come unto Me * * and I will give you rest." That is your line of prayer and labor. Man, woman, whatever your sphere and condition of life, be it joy or grief, health or sickness, household worries or community persecutions, envious successes or ignominious defeats, your line of prayer and labor is marked. Learn to brave the world. Learn to use the world. Learn to meet the ills and allurements and contradictions of the world with such faith in the support of Christ, with such appropriation of the strength in Christ that you shall yourself be conqueror and more than conqueror.

ADJUSTMENT.

ADJUSTMENT.

"Unto the praise of His glory."—Ephe. i: 14.

The valley views are narrow and hampered. It is a small world that unfolds itself to the common gaze. And as one tarries down amid the narrowness and limitation of the valley a certain interpretation of life that accords with these conditions will result. It becomes a necessity that we make occasional journey to the mountains—that we leave the plain for a season, so that our horizon shall broaden and expand until the eye and the imagination weary of the stretch. What marvellous changes are wrought in the life by such experience. We have been leading a life of details and pettinesses— we have been hemmed in by hills and circumstances, and now it is determined that we ascend some Himalaya height that shall correct our vision, give us a good sweep of landscape and prepare us for truer measurement of the world. So we stand on the summit of the mountain. We have severed ourselves from the distant, meagre, restricted, uninspiring conditions. The beautiful, endless panorama stretches away into exquisite dimness. We command the sublimity of nature. Miles upon miles of great fields and vast forests, valley after valley, and mountain after mountain, skies that are

immeasurable in compass, the silver threads of
swift-descending streams, and the radiancy of lake-
lets that hide themselves modestly within the covert
of obscure nooks, the curious, changeful play of
shadow and sunshine through the noble vision. Ah!
these words will not paint the view and these words
will not interpret the subtle inspiritment that communicates itself to the observant, sympathetic, ap-
preciative soul. It means enfranchisement to many
a heart. It means newness and largeness of plan,
thought, experience. And that is the history of
truth-views. We press so near to the things that
concern our prosaic, monotonous living, we restrict
our intimacies so closely to care, pain, tribulation,
worry, we abide so industriously in the valleys of
small vision that we forfeit the majestic conceptions
of truth that contain noble impulses and infinite
potency of good. I ask you to stand with me upon
the Himalaya heights of the divine revelation. I
ask you to gaze with me upon that vast, sublime,
inspiring truth-view indicated by the words, "Unto
the praise of His glory." We want the stimulation
and the exaltation that are fathered by occasional
mountain top visions of truth.

Note first the theatre. "In the beginning God
created the heavens and the earth." This were
to the praise of His glory. "The heavens declare
the glory of God and the firmament sheweth His
handiwork. Day unto day uttereth speech and night
unto night sheweth knowledge. There is no speech

nor language; their voice cannot be heard. Their line is gone out through all the earth, and their words to the end of the world. In them hath He set a tabernacle for the sun, * * whose going forth is from the end of the heaven, and his circuit unto the ends of it; and there is nothing hid from the heat thereof."—Psalm xix. This were "to the praise of His glory." As one gazes into the systems of the universe, as one makes effort to count the myriad hosts of suns which centre their own satellites, as one measures our little planet and then multiplies its bulk and motion and law by the infinite mathematics of Jehovah—it is not a difficult task to translate these things into a phrase of such magnitude as "unto the praise of His glory." But we have to do with small part of this infinite universe. Our scope of vision is very circumscribed. The theatre narrows itself to this little world. But the gaze which we put upon *it* quickens us into awe and adoration. What beautiful and splendid stage for the evolution of human nature! Did you ever give long and earnest thought to the variety, delicacy, richness, perfection, beauty, multiplicity of design evidenced in the world? It must be appropriate theatre with all the many and needful accessories to a full, regal, complex life. So nature is fashioned after the divine idea. "And God saw that it was good." Outlines, colors, forms, combinations—they were all ordained so that they should truly minister to mind, and they were wrought into

G

divine landscapes. Mountains, seas, plains, valleys,
rivers, Arctic ices and Tropic breezes, they were set
to do his bidding and serve the grand finale of the
earth mission. Verdant fields, blossomful gardens,
curious foliage, fruitful vines, they are made as
loyal helpers, contributing their allotment to the
ravishment of earth. And when life throbs
through all the realm and this paradise invites to
its riches and its splendors, when brilliant insects
fling their beauteousness into the sunshine, and birds
freight the air with rarest music, and flowers, trees,
beasts, skies, landscapes, do homage to the wise
Creator, shall we not join our glad acclaim and
say "unto the praise of His glory?" "The earth is
the Lord's and the fullness thereof. The world and
they that dwell therein. For he hath founded it
upon the seas and established it upon the floods.
*   *   Lift up your heads, O ye gates; and be ye
lifted up, ye everlasting doors; and the king of
glory shall come in. *   *   Who is this king of
glory? The Lord of hosts, he is the king of glory."
—Psalm xxiv. This is the theatre "Unto the praise
of His glory."

We note the *dramatis personæ*. Who *are* the persons of the drama? And God said, "Let us make
man in our image, after our likeness; and let them
have dominion over the fish of the sea, and over the
fowl of the air, and over the cattle, and over all the
earth, and over every other creeping thing that
creepeth upon the earth. So God created man in

his own image—in the image of God created he him ; male and female created he them."—Gen. i: 26–27. A race is born into the world. Tribes and peoples and nations are begotten. Men and women with unreckonable dispositions, diversities, characteristics, opportunities, experiences, histories. These are the actors. " Unto the praise of His glory." And they are a curious multitudinous host —these persons of the drama. They are immortal spirits, and they wear mortal bodies. This garment of flesh is the palpable and insistent thing that first obtrudes itself upon notice. " I will praise thee," sings David, "for I am fearfully and wonderfully made."—Psal. cxxxix: 14. Even this body seems to say, " Unto the praise of His glory." " Christ shall be magnified in my body," says Paul—Phil. i: 24. " What ! know ye not that your body is the temple of the Holy Ghost which is in you, which ye have of God, and ye are not your own ? For ye are bought with a price ; therefore, glorify God in your body. * * I. Cor. vi : 19–20. A physical nature is knitted for a season to the spiritual nature. But the physical nature was adjusted deftly, wisely, helpfully to the spiritual. This body, with all its intricate, multiform machinery, was designed to serve the purposes of the spirit. It was not made to trammel us, or distress us, or perplex us, or destroy us. The marvelous, beautiful anatomy was fashioned into an apt and generous responsiveness to the will of the spirit. " Unto the praise of His glory."

Although this body is the obtrusive factor in the man composition, it is the heart, mind, spirit that receive chief emphasis. Here it is that we image our creator. And what field for illustration in respect to the praise of God's glory! We count it notable achievement when Handel writes his oratorio and guides the great organ and the many varied choir into the melodious, majestic rendition of it. A thousand and a million notes are woven into a perfect web of rarest music. And the oratorio pours its regal, joyous way into the souls of men with all the wealth of its precious inspiritment. We count it a notable achievement for Handel. And we quicken with admiration and reverence when we study some great harmonious, artistic structure like St. Peter's Church. What masterful genius swayed the rugged body and sensitive spirit of Michael Angelo? Did man design and execute this temple of beauty? Mosaics and statues, pillared aisles and frescoed ceilings, gorgeous draperies and noble paintings, sculptured arches and bronzed portals, all wrought with a symmetry of thought and a melodiousness of expression that are superlative! We make obeisance to such mind. And how we glow with fervid enthusiasm when we sit us down before the work of Shakespeare, and quench our great thirst at this inexhaustible fountain of truth, and yield us to the magic of that spirit which sways the mind of the world! We speak our mighty words of loyal appreciation, and they seem tame and worthless. Ah! these creators of art, music, literature, they amaze and thrill us with their precious evidences of mastery and genius. Their great works stimulate men to an earnestness and emulation that are full of good promise and profitable issue. But who made Handel, Angelo, Shakespeare? There is a Supreme creative mind that fathers all genius, ability, life. And these achievements, which come as the consummate flower of manhood, are simply phrasings of our theme, "Unto the praise of His glory."

And there is the heart work. It opens to us the richest things of the world experience. A sweet sensitiveness to the ministry of nature, of men, of God, that gives fresh scope to the life powers. We are made in the divine image. It is love that now throbs its answer back to love. It were enough to move a man into richest transports, this force, and enterprise, and impulse of human affection. You see the mother bending over the helpless babe; love graces every movement and expression. That mother would yield her life for the sake of the little one. You meet David and Jonathan tied into a oneness that sorrow, conflict, terror, defeat, cannot break or destroy. Or it is the union of husband and wife. Vicissitudes of fortune are many. Sickness, disappointment, ruin, separation, infamy, duty, death—they may work their mission and gloom the life but love yields not one whit of service, confidence, devotion. It triumphs over all difficulties and never meets rebuke or defeat. Perhaps it is affection that centres in some special class of men. The love of soldier for comrade and commander, the love of workman for his true, strong leader, the love of missioner for the poor, the lost, the depraved, the love of Great-heart for the company of the rebellious—it matters not. It is all witness to this mighty, palpitant, resistless love-nature that reflects the heart of the Almighty. And God who is love, hath made us in His own image.   ·

But why should we particularize? These are the persons of the drama. Men and women, served by physical nature, endowed with splendid gifts of intellect and affection, immortal spirits, born with an individuality that is unique. And these persons of the drama, a great, countless, shifting motley company, find a world the theatre for their movement.

And now we name the drama. It is called Redemption. It was all in the mind of the Creator ere time was differenced from eternity. " According as He hath chosen us in Him before the foundation of the world, that we should be holy and without blame before Him in love."—Eph. i: 4. The theatre is prepared. The persons of the drama begin their entrances. The first parents are sharing the joys of Eden. It is a matter of self-determination. They are free to do their will, and God puts upon them the divine obligation of obedience. They choose to eat of the tree of good and evil. Paradise is suddenly gloomed. " They heard the voice of the Lord God walking in the garden in the cool of the day." They face the curse. They are expelled from Eden. The first act of this mighty world drama is concluded.

What endless task of human conquest lies before this race of men ! Who dare voice any hope ? Lo the very curse treasures the germ of infinite blessing. " It shall bruise thy head and thou shalt bruise his heel." But the race multiplies, waxes wicked and presumptuous. " And God saw that the wickedness of man was great in the earth, and that every imagination of the thoughts of his heart was only evil continually." The flood came. The second act of this great world drama is concluded.

The bow of promises guides men into better hoping. Abraham is called. " In thee shall *all* the families of the earth be blessed."—Gen. xii: 3. We look into the eastern horizon and we detect the signs of the gray dawning. Moses appears. The Lord summons him to leadership. God said unto Moses, " I am that I am ;" " Go." The chosen people are guided into the Promised Land. God makes them pause by Sinai and communicates the Law. The nation then begins its strange, adventurous, checkered, eventful narrative. Judges, generals, kings, prophets, priests, they all share the responsibilities of authority. They all pursue their diverse, antago-

nistic, loyal or rebellious courses.   But the promise
of some great deliverer stirs the entire national
life.   When David attains the sovereignty he does
not rest in his achievement as the goal of Hebrew
mastership.   He sings his song of hopefulness.
"The Lord said unto my Lord, 'Sit thou at my
right hand, until I make thine enemies thy foot-
stool.   The Lord shall send the rod of thy strength
out of Zion.'"—Psalms cx: 1-2.   And then comes
the large company of prophet workmen, rebuking
Israel, counselling Israel, encouraging Israel ; all
their mission converging in some statement concerning the Messiah.   Isaiah voices the prophecy with
tenderest pathos when he recites how "He hath
borne our griefs and carried our sorrows"; * * how
"He was wounded for our transgressions, He was
bruised for our iniquities."—Isai. liii: 5.   And Jeremiah continues the message of triumph—xxiii :
5 and 6—"Behold, the days come, saith the Lord,
that I will raise unto David a righteous Branch, and
a king shall rule and prosper, and shall execute
judgment and justice in the earth ; * * and this
is His name whereby He shall be called, the Lord
our Righteousness."   The world gets weary with
its waiting.   Nations seek the light with prayer-
ful fervency.   Vice, sin, crime, riot through the
earth.   Israel itself becomes the servitor of pagan
Rome.   The most shameless debauches and the
most horrible crimes count for little—so thoroughly
is conscience seared and the nobler nature crushed.
The third act of the drama is concluded.

The fourth act comes apace. The Star of Bethlehem appears. It betokens the desire of nations. "And suddenly there was with the angel a multitude of the heavenly host praising God, and saying, ' glory to God in the highest, and on earth peace, good-will toward men.'"—Luke ii: 13 and 14. It is the entrance of the central character. "And thou shalt call His name Jesus. For He shall save the people from their sins." How gentle and modest this divine man! His early years pass away amid obscurity. In the fullness of time he enters upon the appointed public achievement. Miracle, instruction, example, authority, leadership, they tell the course. Temptation, submission, transfiguration, crucifixion, resurrection, ascension; what magnitude of work—what majesty and significance of life are compressed into these brief years! "And the clouds received Him out of sight." He said unto the disciples, " thus it was written and thus it behooved Christ to suffer and to rise from the dead the third day, and that repentance and remission of sins should be preached in His name among all nations ; * * "And it came to pass while He blessed them He was parted from them and carried up into heaven." And thus is concluded the fourth act of this drama of Redemption.

The true hearts tarry at Jerusalem. The Holy Ghost descends. The teachers are scattered through the nations. "I will draw all men unto me." The fifth act of the mighty drama opens. The fall of man, the ruin of the race, the struggle of the nations, the sacrifice of Christ—they precede the great, last act. The work of regeneration and rejuvenation begins at Jerusalem. First, it is the little company of disciples; then a larger company of citizens; then bands of neighbor people; then scattered churches of Palestine; then multiplied Stations through the Roman empire; then at last the empire itself in all its mighty reach of power and splendor. The centuries come and go. Eighteen and nearly nineteen of them are wrought into history. The banner of the cross appears in Europe. It passes into Africa; it pushes its way through the waters and glorifies the new born nations of the western continent. It continues its progress of triumph until it declares its message amid the isles of the sea. The whole earth becomes girded with this soldier-service of Christ. Millions upon millions march to the music of the Christian hope. Men, tribes, nations, swing into the majestic line. "He whose right it is shall reign." "All hail the power of Jesus' name." Earth redeemed, the race regenerated, man schooled into the Christian character—"Unto the praise of His glory." Friends, is it not a grand and majestic theatre— this curiously builded world? Is it not a wonderful, myriad-sided company, this human race, the persons of the drama? Is it not a drama of infinite interest, significance, sublimity—this drama of redemption?

And we share the movement. *We* are persons of the drama. What honor is put upon us that we are wrought into this magnificent action which gathers the ages into its compass and issues "unto the praise of His glory!" And this is the mountain top vision of truth. And how it quickens the hero spirit within us! Pain, care, trial, suffering, tribulation, discipline, they are remanded to their rightful places. The repulsiveness and the fearfulness of these things are interpreted into language of generous incitement. Pain—that is subsidiary, essential factor in the massive workmanship of time. Care—that means judicious investment of self in the common labors of men. Worry—that is the small friction of the mind which we divert into channels of faith. Tribulation—that is task of flail and threshing floor with good purpose of fine, clean harvest. Suffering—that is mode of conquest that mirrors the very spirit of Jesus. Discipline—that is the divine procedure which carries infinite potency of personal achievement. Yes, when we stand upon the Himalaya heights and get the large, clear, unobstructed, illimitable view of life and world, trouble subsides into narrow and obscure proportions, and we learn how perfect adjustment is the will and work of God. We will rest us in the comfort and the courage of His word. We will listen to the messages that press us into heroic service. Living a love that centres in Jesus we will be strong to hope "Unto the praise of His glory."

www.ingramcontent.com/pod-product-compliance
Lightning Source LLC
Chambersburg PA
CBHW020802020726
47495CB00008B/2546